SUPERDOODLES

ZOO ANIMALS

WRITTEN AND ILLUSTRATED BY BEV ARMSTRONG

The Learning Works

The Learning Works

*Editing and Typography by
Kimberley A. Clark*

Library of Congress Catalog Number:
93-080431
ISBN 0-88160-230-2
LW 325

Printed in the United States of America.

Current Printing (last digit):

10 9 8 7 6 5 4 3 2 1

Introduction

SUPERDOODLES are books that provide easy, step-by-step instructions for super line drawings. The zoo animals in this book may be sketched large for murals or posters, or small for bookmarks and flip books. They may be used individually in separate pictures or combined to create scenes of various habitats.

As you follow the steps, draw in pencil. Dotted lines appear in some steps. Make these lines light so that they can be easily erased later. If an animal has lots of stripes or spots, don't worry about copying the markings exactly—no two animals are identical. Finish your drawing by going over it with a colored pencil, crayon, or felt-tipped pen.

If you enjoy this book, look for other **Learning Works SUPERDOODLES**. Titles in this series are *Dinosaurs, Endangered Animals, Mammals, Marine Life, Rain Forest, Reptiles, Sports,* and *Vehicles*.

aardvark

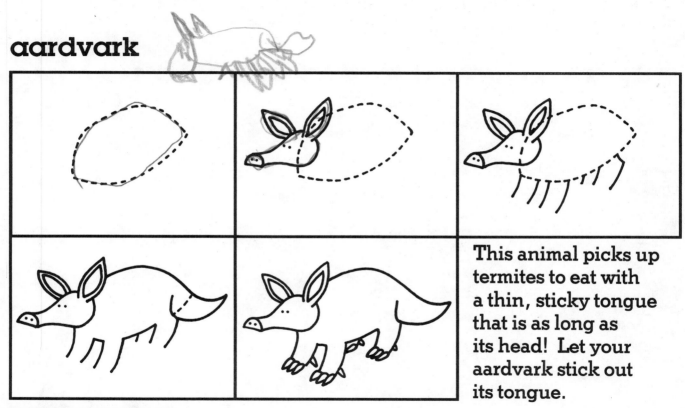

This animal picks up termites to eat with a thin, sticky tongue that is as long as its head! Let your aardvark stick out its tongue.

3

African lion

After sleeping through the heat of the day, lions become active at dusk. Draw a lion silhouetted against an African sunset.

Asian elephant

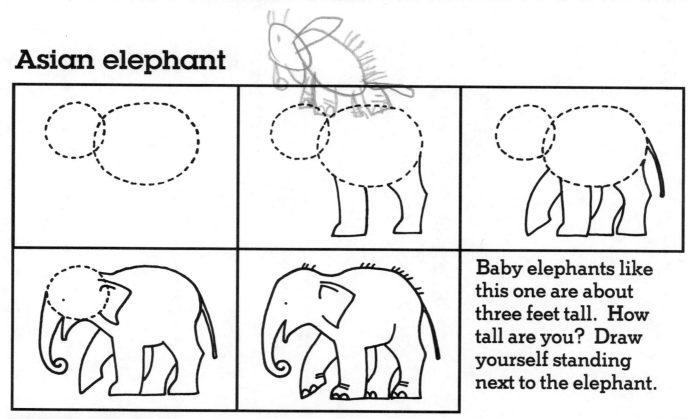

Baby elephants like this one are about three feet tall. How tall are you? Draw yourself standing next to the elephant.

Bactrian camel

Wild Bactrian camels live in high snowy mountains. Their long, shaggy hair protects them from the cold. Draw a Bactrian camel in the snow.

black swan

Draw a swan gliding on a quiet pond. Use tracing paper to copy your swan, and add an upside-down reflection to your drawing.

boa constrictor

These boas produce live babies—up to 50 at a time! Baby boas are about one-eighth as long as the adults. Draw a boa constrictor with some babies.

brindled gnu

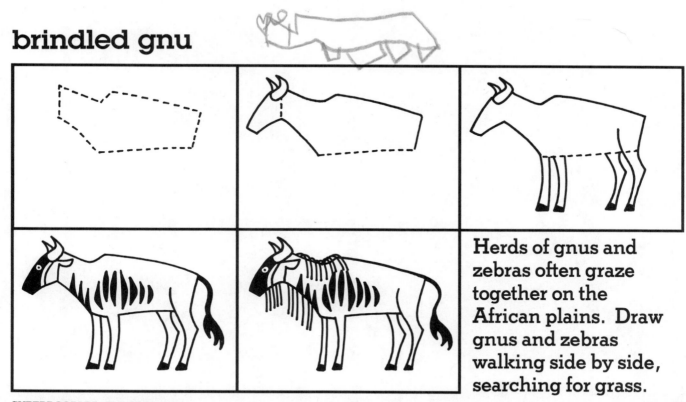

Herds of gnus and zebras often graze together on the African plains. Draw gnus and zebras walking side by side, searching for grass.

celebes tarsier

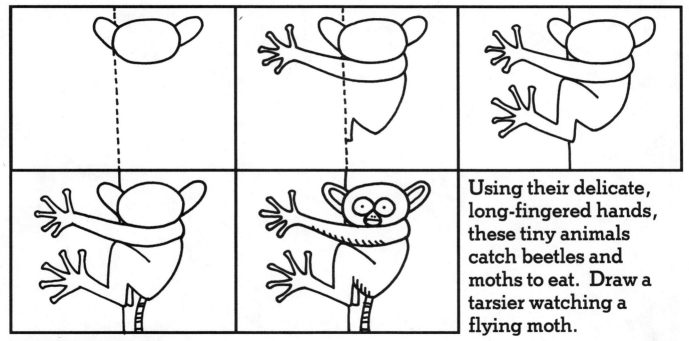

Using their delicate, long-fingered hands, these tiny animals catch beetles and moths to eat. Draw a tarsier watching a flying moth.

chimpanzee

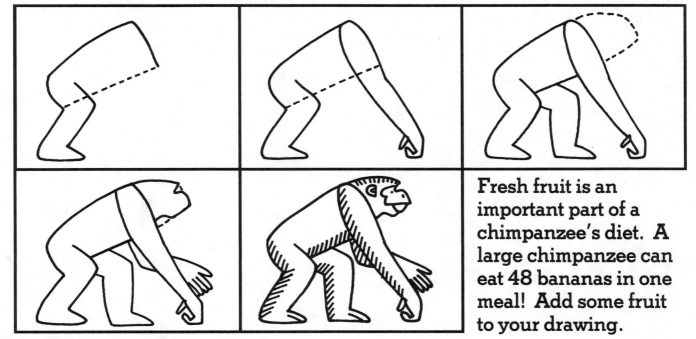

Fresh fruit is an important part of a chimpanzee's diet. A large chimpanzee can eat 48 bananas in one meal! Add some fruit to your drawing.

crowned crane

Cranes gather in small groups to dance, bowing to each other and jumping high in the air. Draw some cranes dancing in the African grasslands.

dart-poison frog

This frog's bright red or yellow color warns other animals that it is poisonous. Draw a squirrel monkey (p. 31) deciding not to eat your frog.

emu

These huge birds are unable to fly but can run 40 miles per hour on their long, strong legs. Draw a herd of emus racing across the Australian plains.

fennec

These desert foxes dig long burrows in which to hide from the sun's scorching heat. Draw a fennec curled up in its sandy tunnel.

Grant's zebra

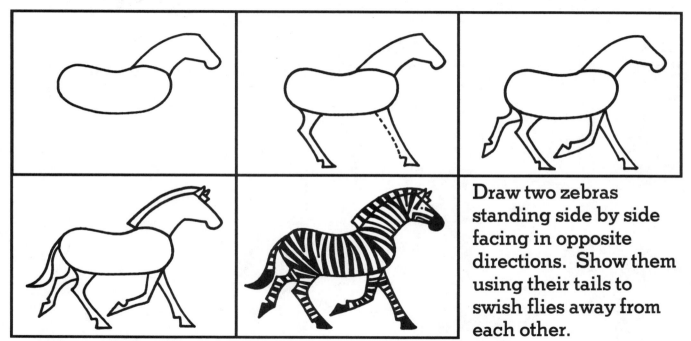

Draw two zebras standing side by side facing in opposite directions. Show them using their tails to swish flies away from each other.

greater flamingo

The flamingo's nest is a small mound of mud on which a single egg is laid. Draw a nest holding an egg that is just beginning to hatch.

great hornbill

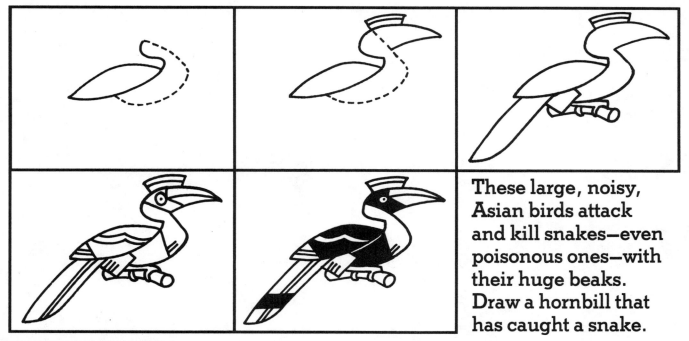

These large, noisy, Asian birds attack and kill snakes—even poisonous ones—with their huge beaks. Draw a hornbill that has caught a snake.

18

hippopotamus

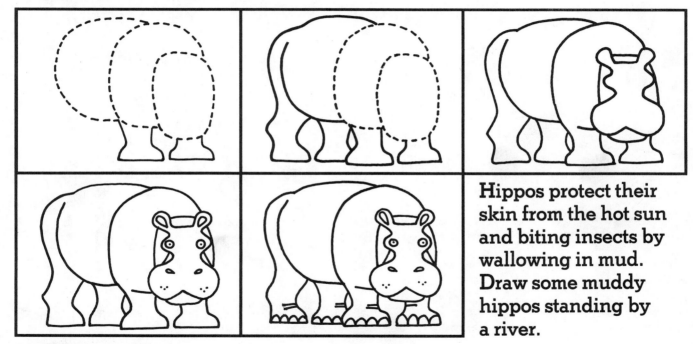

Hippos protect their skin from the hot sun and biting insects by wallowing in mud. Draw some muddy hippos standing by a river.

king vulture

This large, weird bird does not build nests but simply lays one or two eggs among rocks on the ground. Draw a pair of vultures with eggs.

20

lesser panda

These pandas sleep in trees during the day and come down to eat bamboo at dusk. Draw a pair of pandas climbing a tree, sleeping, or eating.

meerkat

Draw a colony of meerkats, with some sitting up straight watching for enemies while others sleep lying on their backs, relaxing in the sun.

Nigerian giraffe

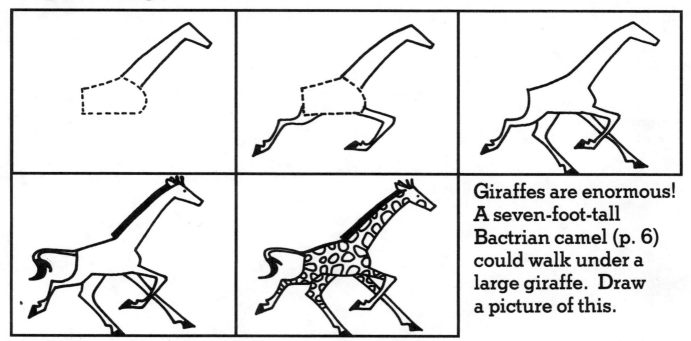

Giraffes are enormous! A seven-foot-tall Bactrian camel (p. 6) could walk under a large giraffe. Draw a picture of this.

Nile monitor

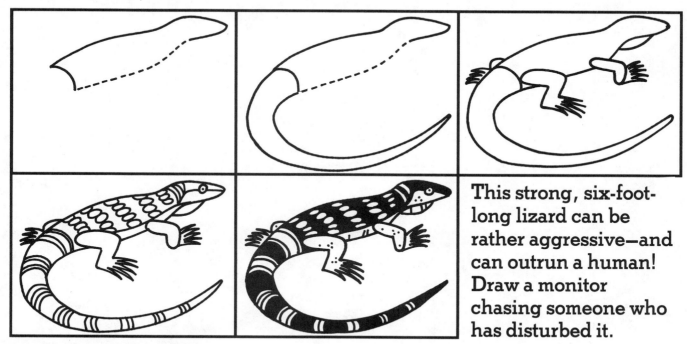

This strong, six-foot-long lizard can be rather aggressive—and can outrun a human! Draw a monitor chasing someone who has disturbed it.

platypus

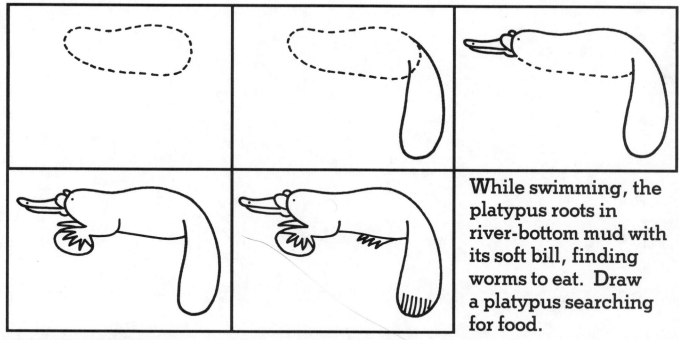

While swimming, the platypus roots in river-bottom mud with its soft bill, finding worms to eat. Draw a platypus searching for food.

25

polar bear

A polar bear's twin cubs each weigh just one pound at birth and stay with their mother for three years. Add two cubs to your drawing.

26

sable antelope

Sable antelope are brown or black with white markings. Using a picture of this handsome animal, design a logo for a zoo or wild animal park.

sea lion

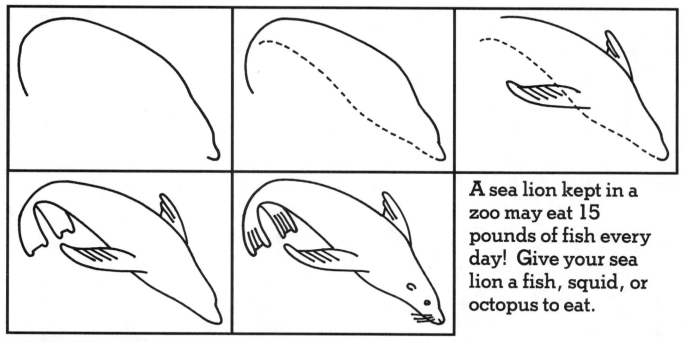

A sea lion kept in a zoo may eat 15 pounds of fish every day! Give your sea lion a fish, squid, or octopus to eat.

28

silvery gibbon

Make several gibbons from construction paper, and hang them on a string stretched across your room.

spectacled bear

Many problems are caused by zoo visitors who give snacks to the animals. Use your drawing to make a poster that says "Please don't feed me!"

squirrel monkey

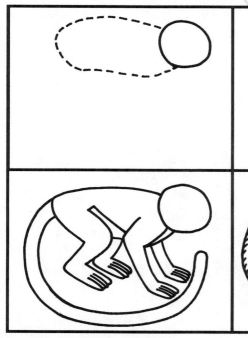

This monkey has a body 12 inches long and a 16-inch-long tail. On a large piece of paper, draw a life-size squirrel monkey.

wallaroo

Wallaroos, also known as rock kangaroos, live among rocks where they are camouflaged by their gray-brown fur. Draw a wallaroo in its natural habitat.